MOMO'S KITTEN

BY MITSU AND TARO YASHIMA
PUFFIN BOOKS

Penguin Books Ltd, Harmondsworth, Middlesex, England
Penguin Books, 40 West 23rd Street, New York, New York 10010, U.S.A.
Penguin Books Australia Ltd, Ringwood, Victoria, Australia
Penguin Books Canada Limited, 2801 John Street, Markham, Ontario, Canada L3R 1B4
Penguin Books (N.Z.) Ltd, 182-190 Wairau Road, Auckland 10, New Zealand

First published by The Viking Press 1961
Viking Seafarer Edition published 1971
Published in Puffin Books 1977

5   7   9   10   8   6

Library of Congress Cataloging in Publication Data
Yashima, Mitsu, pseud.   Momo's kitten.
Summary: A little Japanese-American girl finds a stray kitten
and is allowed to keep it as a pet.
1. Cats—Legends and stories. [1. Cats—Fiction.
2. Pets—Fiction] I. Yashima, Taro, pseud., joint author. II. Title.
PZ10.3.Y34Mo7   [E]   76-54746
ISBN 0-14-050200-9

Manufactured in the United States
by Lake Book/Cuneo, Inc., Melrose Park, IL

Set in Goudy Modern

To Momo
who now wants to be
a veterinarian

Momo's family moved out West from New York City to Los Angeles, but Momo did not see any ranches or cowboys around her.

Instead of these, on the way home from the nearby market one afternoon she found a miserable kitten under a geranium bush by the sidewalk.

"If your father says it's all right, you may keep the kitty," Mother said. Momo made herself ready to cry in case Father should say it was not all right. And when Father smiled,

seeing Momo with a kitty in her arms, she held the kitty tight and whispered,
"Oh, you are my Nyan-Nyan!" That is the name small children call kittens in Japan.

Nyan-Nyan was a gentle-natured kitten and became cleaner and rounder every day.

Only once Nyan-Nyan turned over the canary cage, and that was all.

That summer, Momo went to stay in a camp in the mountains and she missed her kitty.
But whenever her parents visited camp, Nyan-Nyan came with them to see Momo.

On their last visit Momo's mother told her, "Nyan-Nyan is not a Nyan-Nyan any more. She's going to have kittens."

One early autumn morning Nyan-Nyan became a mother. Five tiny Nyan-Nyans

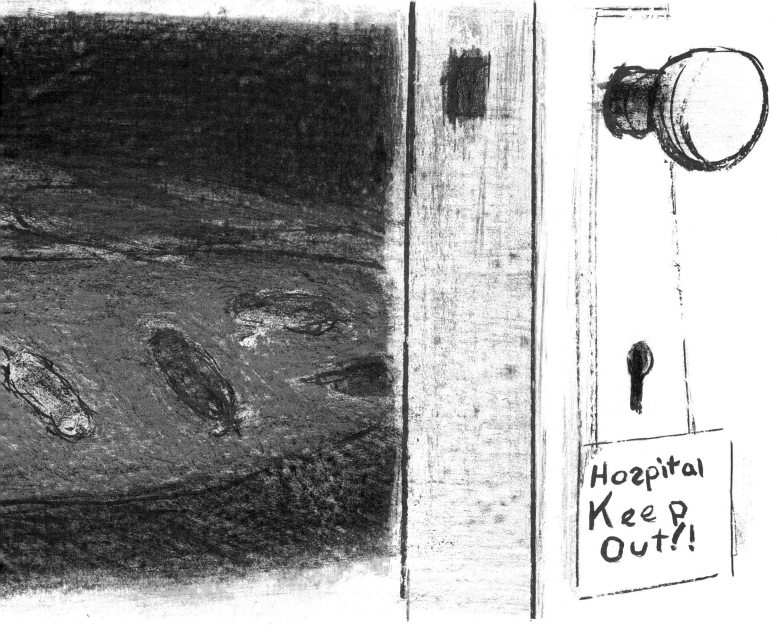

Hozpital Keep Out!!

were born on Momo's car coat, which she had spread for them the night before.

The tiny Nyan-Nyans could not walk at all and drank milk from their mother all day and night long. Mother Nyan-Nyan often gave each one a bath by licking its whole body.

When they were picked up, they kept their tongues moving as if they were still
drinking milk in the air.

Every day, on the way home from school, Momo's classmates came up to see the kittens.

Mother Nyan-Nyan did not like so many children watching, making noise, and touching her kittens. She tried often to move her family to where nobody could bother them.

Soon the five kittens became strong enough to begin to walk. Just as none of them were alike in the marking of their fur, so no two characters were alike.

Some of them learned what cows' milk is, and they grew bigger than the rest, who did not care about it.

The bigger ones were good at climbing the fence, and the smaller ones were good at jumping over things.

Some of them were interested in chasing flies or insects, and some were interested in chasing their own tails.

Each one showed his interest in something different.

There was one that liked to climb up Momo's panda to pull its tongue.

Sometimes all of them were interested in sleeping in the same salad bowl.

There was one that started to sleep in the pigeon cage on the balcony.

Momo began to dream of having not only these kittens but many other animals
in her home.

But the kitchenette was too small to keep even five kittens. They had to be kept on the balcony.

Not only that, they had to be given away to Momo's parents' friends.

After the first kitten was taken away Momo felt like crying, though the boy next door had a different view. "Oh, if your home is a zoo, it will smell terrible!" Momo did not want that.

So to console herself, when each kitten left home, Momo made a decorated certificate.

Pedro was the father's name on these certificates. Pedro belonged to the girl next door, and Momo imagined he was the father of the five kittens.

Soon Mother's Day of that year came. Momo made the breakfast for the first time in her life and carried it in to her mother.

Also Momo did not forget to carry another breakfast which she made for the first time in her life, to the mother of five kittens.

Now the most miserable kitty of a year ago was the most beautiful mother cat in the whole world.

The most beautiful mother cat in the whole world was expecting again.